Put Beginning Readers on the Right Track with ALL ABOARD READING™

The All Aboard Reading series is especially for beginning readers. Written by noted authors and illustrated in full color, these are books that children really and truly *want* to read—books to excite their imagination, tickle their funny bone, expand their interests, and support their feelings. With four different reading levels, All Aboard Reading lets you choose which books are most appropriate for your children and their growing abilities.

Picture Readers—for Ages 3 to 6
Picture Readers have super-simple texts with many nouns appearing as rebus pictures. At the end of each book are 24 flash cards—on one side is the rebus picture; on the other side is the written-out word.

Level 1—for Preschool through First Grade Children
Level 1 books have very few lines per page, very large type, easy words, lots of repetition, and pictures with visual "cues" to help children figure out the words on the page.

Level 2—for First Grade to Third Grade Children
Level 2 books are printed in slightly smaller type than Level 1 books. The stories are more complex, but there is still lots of repetition in the text and many pictures. The sentences are quite simple and are broken up into short lines to make reading easier.

Level 3—for Second Grade through Third Grade Children
Level 3 books have considerably longer texts, use harder words and more complicated sentences.

All Aboard for happy reading!

To Emily, a wonder woman too—S.A.K.

Photo credits: pp. 14 and 37, AP/Wide World Photos; p. 25 and back cover, Brian J. Myers; p. 48, Brian Myers/Photo Run.

Library of Congress Cataloging-in-Publication Data

Kramer, Sydelle.
    Wonder women / by S. A. Kramer ; illustrated by Jim Campbell.
        p.   cm.—(All aboard reading. Level 3)
        1. Women athletes—Biography—Juvenile literature.   I. Campbell, Jim, ill.
II. Title. III. Series.
GV697.A1K73 1997
796.092'2—dc21
    [B]   97-11023
                                                                                                   CIP
                                                                                                   AC

ISBN 0-448-41722-7 (GB)   A B C D E F G H I J
ISBN 0-448-41589-5 (pbk)   A B C D E F G H I J

ALL
ABOARD
READING™

Level 3
Grades 2-3

WONDER WOMEN

of Sports

By S. A. Kramer
Illustrated by Jim Campbell

With photographs

Grosset & Dunlap • New York

Water Woman

Atlanta, Georgia. The 1996 Olympic Games. The 100-meter freestyle is almost over. Amy Van Dyken is behind—but she's not giving up. This is her first Olympic event, and she wants to do well. Twenty-three-year-old Amy has a dream—to take home a gold medal.

Just a few meters to go. Amy strokes furiously. Her head's so low in the water, fans see only her cap. She's tired, but somehow she turns up the speed. Amy always gives everything she's got.

This time it's not enough. Amy finishes fourth. No gold, no silver—not even a bronze. But as she leaves the pool, she isn't thinking about losing. Her burst of speed has made her muscles cramp. The pain is so bad, she can't even stand.

Amy falls to the pool deck. Cramps shoot into her back and neck. She gasps for air. Trainers have to carry her off on a stretcher.

What a way to start the Olympics! Amy can't believe her bad luck. But it's not the first time her health has gotten in her way.

Ever since she was little, Amy's had asthma (you say it like this: AZ-mah). Asthma is an illness that makes it hard to breathe. Amy's lungs have never worked right.

As a child, she was always out of breath. Climbing just one flight of stairs left her huffing and puffing. But when she was seven, her doctor said swimming might help her. So Amy headed straight for the pool.

Her talent didn't show right away—far from it. Even at twelve, she could hardly finish a race. She'd often have to stop in the middle to catch her breath.

Things weren't much better in high school. Amy coughed all the time. She was also awkward, skinny—and six feet tall! Her classmates made fun of her. Amy felt like a nerd.

Somehow she made the school swim team. But then the coach put her on a relay with three other girls.

The girls weren't happy. They complained to the coach. To get Amy to quit, they threw her clothes into the pool. Once they even spat at her.

Amy felt awful. But she didn't leave the team. Later she said, "I'm really stubborn. If someone tells me I stink, I'm going to try to prove them wrong." She vowed that one day she'd make those girls respect her.

In college at Colorado State, Amy joined the swim team. Fighting her asthma, she got all the way to the 1990 junior nationals. But she wasn't fast enough to make the 1992 Olympic team.

Amy kept trying. She got faster and faster. But in 1993, she flopped in the NCAA championships. And after that, she caught a terrible virus.

Amy was depressed. All her training hadn't made her a champion. She told herself, "This is too hard. I want to be normal." For a few months she quit swimming. But she didn't stay away for long. She missed it too much.

Amy charged back into the pool. She learned to make her starts faster and to stroke with more power. To boost her speed, she kept shaving the hair off her body. She said, "If I miss the hair on my knee, it could cost me a hundredth of a second."

Her all-out attitude paid off. In the
1994 world championships, she won a
bronze medal in the 50-meter freestyle.
The same year, she was named female
NCAA swimmer of the year. Then in
1995, she broke the U.S. records for both
the 50-meter and 50-yard freestyle.

Amy was on a roll. In 1996 she won a place on the Olympic team. This time none of her teammates complained. In fact, she became their leader. Her horrible high school years seemed long ago.

Now she's at the Olympic games, lying on a stretcher. Her teammates are worried. But Amy has come back from worse. She calls herself "the tough girl." Sure enough, two hours later her cramps ease up and she's feeling fine.

Her next race is a relay—the 4x100-meter freestyle. There's no way Amy's going to let her teammates down. She hopes those high school girls are watching their TVs today.

The U.S. wins the gold! The team couldn't have done it without Amy. The very next day she wins the 100-meter butterfly by 1/100th of a second.

And she's still not finished. She takes golds in the 50-meter freestyle and the 4x100-meter medley relay, too. That's four in all! Amy is the first and only American woman ever to win four gold medals in one Olympics.

No one makes fun of Amy anymore. In fact, she's almost too popular. Fans won't leave her alone. At hotels, she uses a fake name so strangers can't keep calling her.

Her asthma still makes her sick. Some days, she has to stay out of the water. When she pushes herself too hard, she ends up in the hospital. Even now, Amy takes medicine three times a day.

She often thinks about her future. She may teach biology, or work with deaf children. But one thing she knows for sure. Swimming will always be part of her life.

Tiny Tumbler

California, 1982. Dominique Moceanu (you say it like this: Mo-chee-AH-nu) is six months old—just a little baby. But her parents have already chosen her career. Both of them used to be gymnasts. They hope Dominique will be one, too.

Dominique's father wants to test how strong she is. One day he gets a clothesline and stretches it across the kitchen. Can his baby girl grip it and hang on?

He lifts Dominique up. She grabs hold with her tiny fists. When he lets her go, she swings easily from the line. She's a natural!

By the time she's four, Dominique is a star in her gymnastics club. By seven, she's in her first competition. People clap for her, and she feels thrilled. She remembers, "That's when I knew I was really hooked."

When she's not practicing gymnastics, Dominique watches it on TV. She has her eye on a coach named Bela Karolyi (you say it like this: Kah-ROLL-ee). Two of his gymnasts have won Olympic gold medals. In a dreamy voice, she says to her parents, "Oh, if only I could train with Bela."

One Thanksgiving, the family takes a trip to Houston, Texas. Dominique's excited—she's never been to Houston. But when they arrive, they don't see any of the sights. They drive straight to a gym.

Dominique's confused. She asks, "What are we doing here?"

"Surprise!" her father yells. The gym is Bela Karolyi's!

Dominique's father has talked to the famous coach. He will give ten-year-old Dominique a tryout. This is her big chance.

Dominique is nervous. She's never had a test like this. She must climb a rope, run across the balance beam, and do all kinds of tumbling. Bela will watch her every move.

Dominique's landings aren't always perfect. Sometimes she slips while she's tumbling. But she has energy and willpower. Bela sees she's a fighter. He agrees to be her coach.

Dominique and her family move to Houston. She feels like she's really on her way. But it turns out Bela is a very tough coach. Dominique's training hours double. The exercises are hard. To learn her routines, she must practice each move thousands of times.

For the first few months, Dominique has trouble sleeping. She's scared. Is she really good enough to be Bela's student?

Dominique's a quick learner. She's willing to work hard to succeed. The other girls in the gym help her. Soon she's doing moves she never could before.

Although she's small and cute as a pixie, she shows Bela she's tough. Even if she's in pain, she smiles and prances. Nothing can stop her from performing. She hangs a poem called "Don't Quit" in her room.

By 1992, Dominique has become the youngest athlete ever to make the U.S. junior gymnastics team. In 1994, she wins the U.S. junior championship. Fans adore her. She loves it when they cheer her on.

Now Dominique's so sure of herself, Bela calls her "Ms. Confidence." She signs autographs, "Dominique Moceanu, 1996 Olympic champion, for sure."

In 1995, Dominique wins the U.S.

national women's gymnastics competition. At thirteen, she's the youngest U.S. champion ever. Besides that, she's the first gymnast to be junior champ one year and national champ the next. After her victory, she says, "I was melting with happiness."

Dominique needs time off. She hasn't had a vacation since she was ten. But there's no time for one now. She must train for the 1996 Olympics in Atlanta.

Practicing harder than ever, Dominique does the ninth grade at home with a tutor. She's in the gym eight hours a day, but still earns A's. Just seventy-two pounds, she watches every bite of food. Once in a while, she allows herself a cookie or a piece of chocolate.

Just before the Olympics, disaster strikes. Dominique hurts her right leg. Now she can't practice. Her leg won't heal completely before the competition starts. But the U.S. team wants her anyway.

Dominique is thrilled. She heads for Atlanta. Gabbing and cracking jokes, she doesn't let on how hurt she is. When she gets to Atlanta, she tells reporters, "The doctors said there's going to be a lot of pain . . . but, you know, this is it: the Olympics."

On July 23rd, she and her teammates take the floor. It's the team finals—time for their showdown with the Romanians and the Russians. Over 32,000 fans yell and cheer.

Dominique beams her dazzling smile at the crowd. Her hair is in a ponytail. She's got two earrings in each of her ears. For luck, she's stuck seven guardian angel pins on her gym bag.

Her first event is the uneven parallel bars. She's never liked this routine. But tonight it doesn't matter. She's in the spotlight she loves. And there's a gold medal at stake.

On the bars, Dominique's close to perfect. She's even better on the balance beam, her favorite. She may be in pain, but she's helping her team win.

Her floor exercises are terrific. But her leg gives her trouble on the vault. Will the U.S. still take the gold?

Yes! For the first time in Olympic history, an American women's gymnastics team has won a gold medal. Fans call Dominique and her teammates The Magnificent Seven.

Now Dominique is looking forward to the next Olympics. There's more gold to be won—and she's going after it.

All-American

Southwick, Massachusetts 1983.
Rebecca Lobo stares sadly at the floor.
She's standing at her fifth-grade teacher's
desk, getting scolded. But she can't figure
out what she's done wrong.

Rebecca is a good student. She's also
a tomboy who plays all kinds of sports.
At lunch in the cafeteria, she eats with
the boys. The tallest kid in her class,
she dresses like the boys too.

Her teacher doesn't like that. She
wants Rebecca to act like a girl. No more

pants in class, she orders—only dresses. Rebecca can't play sports with the boys anymore. She must change her ways.

Rebecca says nothing. She just goes back to her seat. But when she gets home, she tells her mom what happened.

Her mom is furious at the teacher. She tells Rebecca a girl should be free to be anything she wants. Above all, she says, Rebecca must be herself. Today, Rebecca says, "I knew then that there was nothing wrong with who I was."

Rebecca keeps dressing the way she wants. And she doesn't give up sports. Her favorite game is basketball. She's been playing since she was four. That's when she saw her brother shoot hoops in the driveway. Rebecca says, "I just wanted to do what he did."

There isn't even a girls' basketball team in her school, so she joins the boys' team. Her coach predicts she'll grow up to be a great athlete. Ten-year-old Rebecca dreams of playing for the NBA's Boston Celtics.

By the time she starts high school, Rebecca's terrific on the court. In her first game, she scores thirty-two points. But off the court, she feels clumsy. She's the tallest kid in the whole school. She doesn't go out on many dates.

Basketball helps her relax. If she's angry or nervous, she just shoots hoops. She leaves the world behind.

The hours of practice pay off. By the time she graduates, Rebecca's the leading scorer, male or female, in the history of Massachusetts high schools.

At the University of Connecticut, she makes the team right away. Everyone there knows she was a big high school star. A lot is expected of her. It makes her nervous. When she first takes the court, her coach says Rebecca is "bad enough for two people."

For the next two years, Rebecca struggles. She doesn't get along with the coach. He tells her she isn't keeping her mind on the game. More and more nervous, she doesn't even like to practice anymore.

But she's popular with her classmates. A good student, she gets high grades. And she begins to feel more confident.

Then in 1993, she finally figures out what the coach wants. Everything falls into place. Rebecca becomes a star.

Six-foot-four, 180 pounds, Rebecca's a great passer with a deadly hook shot. Playing forward or center, she pulls down the rebounds and blocks shots. She's good on offense and defense, and she never hogs the ball.

Soon she becomes the leader of her team, the Huskies. Now her coach has just one problem with her playing style— Rebecca's too nice. He wants her to take more shots and get tough with other teams.

Rebecca listens. The Huskies win game after game. Fans swarm the arena and nickname her LoboCop. They know they're watching the greatest team player in women's basketball.

Before each game, Rebecca's roommate braids her hair for good luck. Soon girls in the stands start to braid their hair exactly the same way. Kids of all ages pass her flowers on the court. Boys and girls, men and women, line up for her autograph. When she goes for a haircut, fans grab her brown locks off the floor.

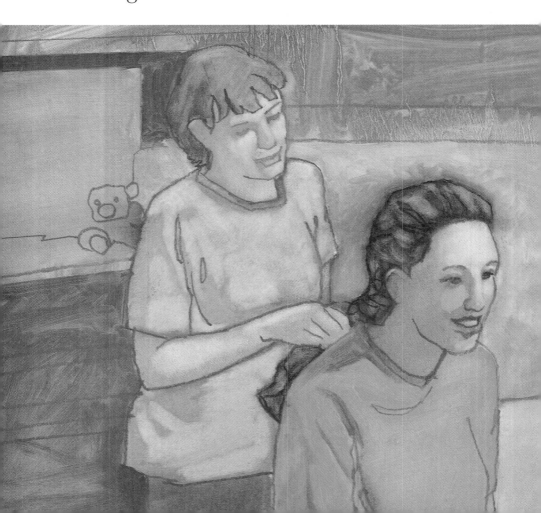

In Rebecca's last year with the Huskies, they win every single game. They're America's only undefeated big college team, male or female. But Rebecca feels their perfect record won't mean much without the 1995 National Collegiate Athletic Association (NCAA) championship. She wants more than anything to win that.

The Huskies go all the way to the NCAA finals. The last game is close. With just seconds left, the Huskies' lead is only three points. Rebecca's on the foul line.

She must make two foul shots, or the other team can come back and win the game.

She bounces the ball and looks up at the rim. Then she makes her shot. It's a basket! Her teammates mob her. But can Rebecca do it again?

She bends her long legs. She holds the ball near her ear. At last she fires. Swish! LoboCop comes through again.

The Huskies go on to win. Fans cheer wildly. Rebecca and her teammates hug and dance. As the band plays, they lift their coach to their shoulders.

The Huskies end their year 35–0. Rebecca is named the finals' Most Valuable Player (MVP). It's a great finish to her college career. She's the only player in Big East history to have over a thousand points and a thousand rebounds. Best of all, she and her teammates have made women's basketball a popular sport.

In 1995, Rebecca wins six different awards for best woman athlete of the year. She jogs with the President and goes on "The Late Show with David Letterman." Her hometown even names a street after her.

And in the summer of 1996, she adds an Olympic gold medal in women's basketball to her other awards.

Now Rebecca plays for the New York Liberty pro team in the Women's National Basketball Association. She is sure of herself, on the court and off. But she still remembers the day her fifth-grade teacher tried to make her give up sports. It's a good thing Rebecca didn't listen.

Flying Feet

Autumn, 1988. Gail Devers is sick. She feels weak, and her head hurts. Sometimes she can't see out of one eye. Sometimes she shakes all over. Her hair is falling out. She forgets even simple things.

Gail isn't eating much. Yet she puts on twenty-four pounds in two weeks. All at once she loses the weight—and gains it right back again.

What's happening to Gail?

A few months ago, this twenty-two-year-old Californian was a track star at UCLA. She set the U.S. record in the 100-meter hurdles. Then she made the 1988 U.S. Olympic team. Experts agreed Gail was someone to watch.

With her long strides, she could run at a speed of almost twenty-five miles an hour. She ran to win, but she always raced fair. Gail was so nice, she asked rivals to take a victory lap with her.

Once her energy seemed endless. Now she can't win a race. She tries to keep training, but she no longer has the strength.

No one can figure out what's wrong. Doctor after doctor—thirteen of them!— tell her she's just tired and nervous. "I thought I was going crazy," Gail says.

Gail takes time off to rest. After a year, she still can't run. Even her friends think her track career is over. But Gail won't give up. She visits one last doctor, and he figures out her problem.

Gail has Graves' disease. That means a gland in her neck makes too much of a certain chemical. The chemical is making her sick. A special treatment called radiation will make her better.

Once she starts the treatments, Gail heads right for the track. She can't wait to run again. But soon her feet hurt. She gets blisters on her heels and between her toes. The blisters fill up with blood.

Gail says her feet feel like they're "going to fall off." None of her doctors knows what's wrong.

Still, Gail keeps running. She wears five pairs of sock to pad her feet. It doesn't help. Every time she leaves the track, her feet are bleeding. Soon they puff up like balloons.

By March, 1991, Gail can barely walk. Her parents move into her apartment to take care of her. Her father carries her from room to room. Her mother gives her baths.

Finally one doctor figures out the problem. The radiation treatments are burning Gail's feet. The mystery is solved in the nick of time. A few more days, and the burns would never have healed. The doctor would have had to cut off both of Gail's feet.

The treatments are changed. Gail starts to feel better. By April, she's walking again. In June, she amazes fans by winning a big race. Then, at the world championships, she takes the silver medal in the 100-meter hurdles. Gail is back!

But she doesn't forget what it was like to be sick. Her illness taught her a lot. She says, "Now I don't feel there's any hurdle in my life I can't get over." But is she healthy enough to beat the world's best track stars?

She is! In the 1992 Olympics, Gail wins the gold medal in the 100-meter dash. Sportswriters call her victory the greatest comeback in track history.

For the next three years, Gail keeps winning. In the 1993 world championships, she becomes the first athlete ever to win both the 100-meter dash and 100-meter hurdles. Then in the 1995 world championships, she finishes first in the 100-meter hurdles.

But none of this matters to her as much as the 1996 Olympics. There, Gail has a chance to make the record books. It's been twenty-eight years since a woman won back-to-back gold medals in the 100-meter dash. It won't be easy, but Gail thinks she can do it.

Most experts laugh at the idea. After all, Gail is twenty-nine years old. She still has to take medicine every day. She must stay on a special diet and get extra sleep.

But Gail believes in herself. She knows she's running well. And she's got her famous "trip finish." That's when she tips her head forward as she reaches the finish line. Some fans think she's about to trip, but she's just leaning over the line.

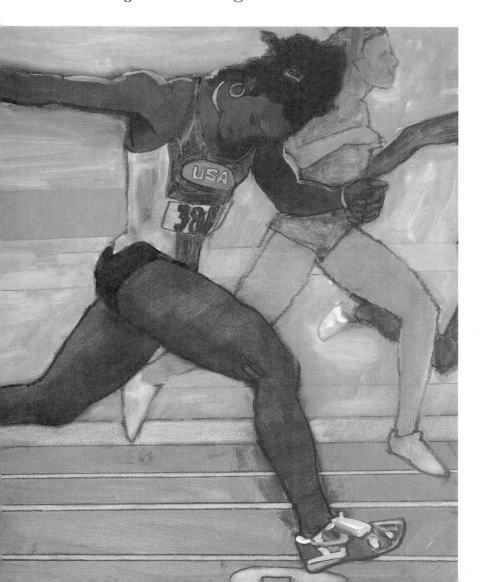

At the Olympics, Gail steps out on the track in style. The scrunchie in her hair matches her uniform perfectly. She's wearing bright lipstick and hoop earrings. Around each wrist is a gold bracelet.

But what fans notice most are Gail's extra-long fingernails. She always paints them different colors. Today's polish is gold, for the medal she plans to win.

The race is on! Eleven seconds later, it's over.

But who won?

It's so close, the judges have to study the video replay.

Gail's the winner!

The trip finish did it. When she hears the news, she jumps into her coach's arms. They twirl around as if they're dancing.

Gail's made sports history. More importantly, she's given fans hope. She beat her illness and never gave up her dream.